THE ADVENTURE OF THE TRIO

EKANSH. N. PAL

Made with ♥ on the Notion Press Platform
www.notionpress.com

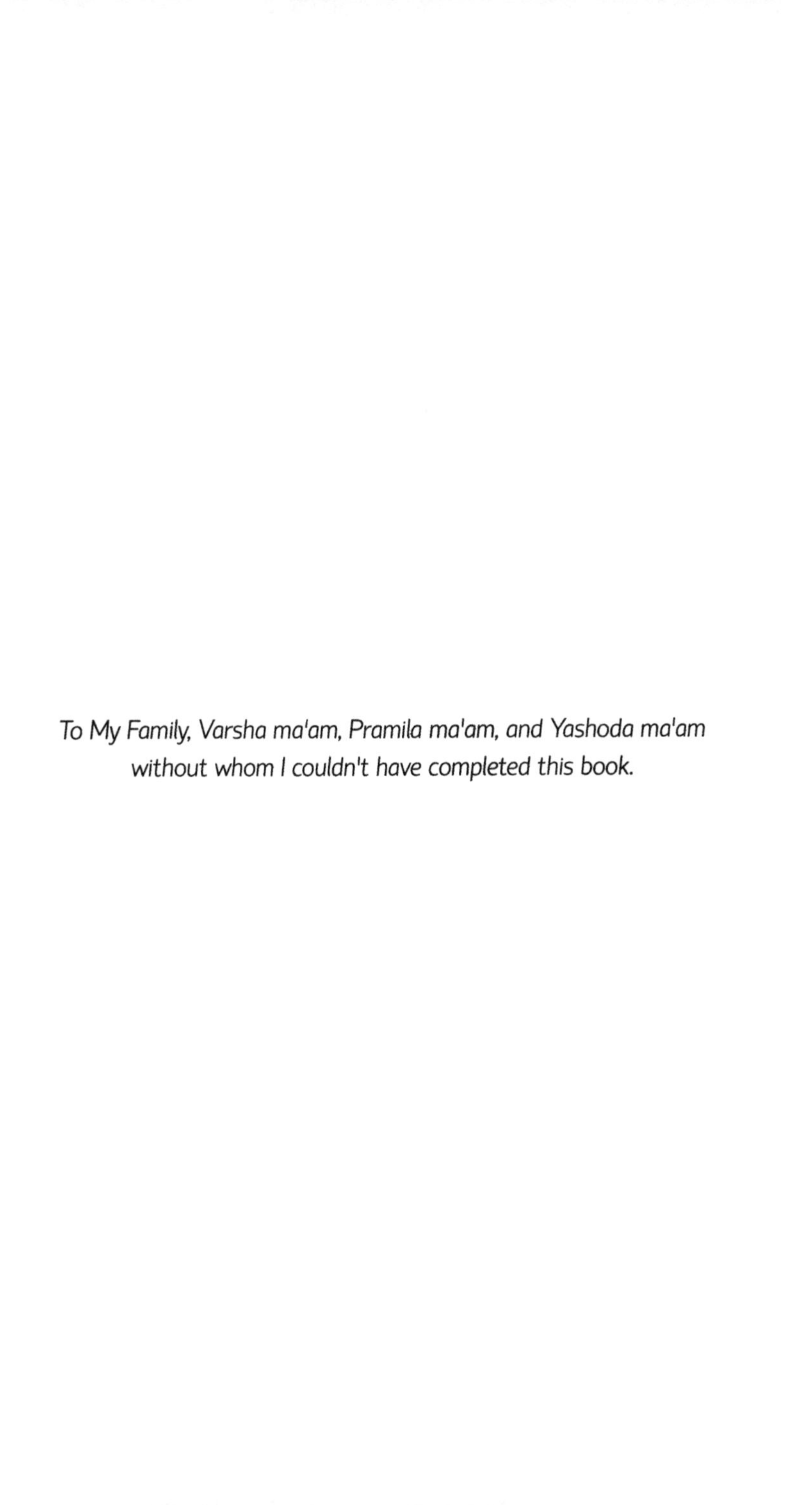

To My Family, Varsha ma'am, Pramila ma'am, and Yashoda ma'am without whom I couldn't have completed this book.

Contents

CHAPTER ONE

Back in Hols

"The best word in the whole world is hols," said Jack, as he gave his sister the lovely buns prepared by the canteen cook. It tasted perfectly good as the earlier food on the usual days was not so good.

"Uncle, it's very tasty", complemented Jack immediately. After eating the delicious buns he rushed to his sister, who was talking with her friends. "Come on otherwise we will miss the train", said Jack, as he led his sister to the small pony trap hired by him. The pony trap was fast as it helped them reach the railway station in time. Jack had a cat's eyes, he located the train easily. As they sat on the train, Jamie said, "I wish I was like you, brother." Jack replied, "It's not necessary and I like you being small." "Alright", said Jamie settling into a nap, while Jack worked out on a novel.

An hour elapsed quickly. The train came to a halt and blew a loud horn, waking up Jamie in fright. "Oh! The train stopped at the station. Hurry up." Jack and his sister quickly came down the train to find mother waiting for them. Her mother, Mrs. Joana was a kind lady loved by the children. There were hugs all around. "Mom! We missed you a heck in the school", cried the children together as they went inside the car.

"Now leave this aside, I have a surprise for you that will be disclosed at home." The children sat quietly till the vehicle reached home.

"Mom, I want some hams", cried Jack. "Get it yourself", said his father. His father, Mr. Jonathan Philpot was a scientist with a frown on his face.

"The secret is that you are going to Palesto castle to live with Mr. Fenturn, my friend. He has opened some hotel or so and needs some customers." "Yippee!" shouted the children as they sped back to their rooms to pack their bags. What happened next was an unforgettable one!

CHAPTER TWO

To Mr. Fenturn

The next morning after a heavy breakfast the children sat in the Limo booked by their father. The children waved to their parents while the limo trundled down the street.

Jim said to the driver "Why Palesto castle is called 'Palesto'. The driver said "Long back ago, probably in the late 1900's, a knight named Palesto ruled here. He was a well known warrior with great skill and courage .During the great war of Tennet, he fell from his horse and was captured alive. He gradually managed to escape and hid here for more than fifty years with his few faithful men. That is why it is very famous and attracts a lot of tourists here."

"Ohhhhhhhh!!" exclaimed the children together. Jack said, "I hope we visit the dungeons soon". "No please no!" cried Jamie as she knew her brother's adventurous attitude. They started talking about castles, goblins, kings and fights. Time passed away. Jack suddenly looked at his watch. He exclaimed, "It's six 'o' clock .It's time for our dinner."Jamie quickly unpacked the sandwiches and they had it in a gulp. After that she took a nap while he read a novel.

Jamie woke up in a fright when the big Limo stopped abruptly. Jack helped his little sister climb down the limo.

"Where is Mr. Fenturn" said Jamie. "There he is," shouted Jack. And indeed he saw a well- dressed man waiting to receive them. "Welcome to Fenturn Inn. I will show your room." he said in his kind voice .The children followed him to the room. It was indeed big for two people.

"Thanks!" said the children politely as he left. "It has been a tiring day." said Jack as he stretched out on the big bed. "Sitting for six hours is no fun." he concluded. "Yeah! I think that too." said Jamie .A minute later they had fallen asleep. They were too sleepy to hear anything.

CHAPTER THREE

Meeting Tobuck and a strange message

Jack woke up at the sound of the church bell ringing. "We'll get late for church," he said waking up his sister, who was in the middle of her sweet dreams. "Oh! I forgot about it. Let's rush to the church. We will miss our prayer." said Jamie jumping out of her bed in surprise.

In a short period, they were ready and were rushing to Mrs. Fenturn, who was a kind lady with a pleasant face. She warmly welcomed them by serving them hot bacon and eggs. They rushed to the church and did their prayers gracefully.

"Let's go the hills for a walk, please" said Jamie. "Ok" said Jack and the two set out towards the hills. They had a pleasant time. Jamie was collecting flowers whereas Jack was taking a stroll. "I have found something" shouted Jack to his sister. And indeed he found something strange.

Meet me on 23rd at PLSO at 9.00PM - H

"Yotta! This is a message that is communicating someone who is probably in need of something. He/she want the person to come on 23rd. I can't understand the last word and the signature.

"Let's rush home, the sun's setting." said Jamie running fast. They soon reached the inn. Mrs. Fenturn said "You're late. But dinner's hot."The children ate to their hearts content.

As they returned to their room, they found a boy younger than Jack resting on the bed. Jack stormed," How dare you enter our room! I will sue you up." The frightened boy ran to his mother, Mrs. Fenturn who said, "Please leave him alone. I'll deal with Tobuck."

Jack thought so, this guy is Tobuck. While they were returning to their room, Jamie said "That guy Tobuck is an 'ok' sort of chap. A talk could solve him." Jack thought the same. He would do it definitely.

CHAPTER FOUR

A walk, talk, and another message

The next morning, Jack and his sister went to Mrs. Fenturn and requested her to send Tobuck with them for a walk .She gladly sent Tobuck with them. The trio went to the nearest summer shop and they had nice time eating snacks and drinking ginger beer.

“You are a good lad but naughtiness makes you bad.” “I try, but I can’t help it” replied Tobuck. “Just don’t show it” said Jack, as he pooled out his pocket money .They were about to leave the shop, when Jack stopped the two. He said “I have a secret to share with you Tobuck. I and Jamie were on a walk on the hill yesterday when we found a secret chit. On it there was a **message** .We couldn’t understand this code **‘P.L.S.O.’** and the signature **‘H’** .What does it mean?”

Tobuck jumped with excitement. “We found a mystery. A real adventure. We will go to the Palesto castle and investigate. **P.L.S.O.** means Palesto and I think H is for Haidi Matar. A famous bomber, who escaped from the prison a fortnight ago. Remember he is going to show up today. Be prepared!

They went back to the inn. Mrs. Fenturn was happy to see her child cheerful. Tobuck went to Jack’s room and the

Trio together did many activities like- playing cards, tic tac toe, catching metal fishes with magnets etc. Time passed by with these activities. Soon it was six '0' clock, time for the dinner. Mrs. Fenturn served them delicious food that they ate till their hearts content. As they wished good night, to her and were about to sleep, they heard a scream.

The trio rushed down to find Mrs. Fenturn screaming "Rat!!" She pointed to the big rat that became the prey of Jack's pocketknife. "A bull's eye." exclaimed Jamie and Tobuck together. They wished good night and went to sleep.

But Jack was awake. As he tried to listen the clock bell ring nine, he looked out of the window. And yes, he could see torch flashes from the Palesto castle. Somebody was signalling. Somebody was hiding there!

CHAPTER FIVE

In Palesto Castle

The next morning the trio went to the Palesto castle with an excuse of a walk. They soon ended in the up castle armed with ropes, torches, and pocketknife. They started hunting all around the castle. Jack was checking the walls; Jamie and Tobuck were checking the ground and roof. Jack heard a great deal of noise behind the wall. Indeed, it looked as if Tobuck was doing a great deal of punching on the wall. "I have found something" shrieked Jamie. The two rushed to see what Jamie had found. They looked at the old piece of linen. A map was drawn inside it. "Whoa! A map." cried the children together.

"It shows hideout of............of Haidi" said, Jack in excitement. I will go tonight to find his hideout." he said bravely . They returned to the inn.

"Let me study the map carefully. You both see it."The trio studied the map carefully. "You see, the bomber could only hide at one place," he said with knowledge. "That is the dungeons. It is not labelled on the map. Probably for safety . I think its entrance begins somewhere near the statue of Charles II. The second entrance is near the castle wall. Well, I'll just focus on one. Enough for me."

"Leave it . Let's enjoy" said Tobuck. After that, they played cards and snap. Time passed by. Soon it was time for dinner. The trio ate hot bacon and eggs . It was time for Jack to go. Jamie prepared him some sandwiches. He packed all the things he needed and was ready for an adventurous night!

CHAPTER SIX

An Adventurous Night

Jack before departing gave a device which he called 'Button –O- Help'. "If I am in danger I will just press the button and the device in your hand will beep."He bid them goodbye and went towards the Palesto castle.

He was soon inside the castle. He hid behind a rock and showed his torch inside the castle. If I am only a kilometer away from the Charles II statue then the dungeons are very near, he thought. He began his hunt.

He took out his shovel and was about to remove the plants when he heard a big piece of stone moving near him. He darted behind his rock. He heard the man move quietly. He saw the man's face threw the man's torchlight.

Yes, It was Haidi. The same eyes. The same zombie-like nose and the same gnome-like ears. He heard him go away. He came out from his rock He went inside the opening. It led to the dungeons. He followed the stairs and reached the place from where the three tunnels began. He chose the middle tunnel in the name of god and continued his journey. The tunnel led to the bomber's [Haidi] hideout.

Yes, he had done it! He went inside and found out that it was a complete storage and home for Haidi. Suddenly, something caught his eye A small iron box. He opened its lid and saw his diary and three to four dynamite. He picked up the diary and began to read it. It stated Haidi's revenge to finish the entire Palesto castle and escape to Iran. Never to be heard again.

As he was about to put the diary in its place, he suddenly got a blow on his nose. It was Haidi.

Jack reacted immediately by punching him on his jawbone Haidi too reacted by giving him a kick in his face. The fight had begun. They fought for a long time. Both of them were not in good condition. Haidi's nose was bleeding. Jack's leg was hurt and he was staggering. He made his final effort and gave a punch with full of force sending his opponent on the floor. Jack dropped on the floor He heard Haidi saying dizzily "Take...... him...... away."

CHAPTER SEVEN

"Jack's not here!!"

The next morning Jamie woke up early. She was thirsty. She looked at Jack's bed. It was empty. She panicked to Tobuck.

Tobuck woke up with a start. Jamie told him that he had not returned. Hearing this, Tobuck was in tension. He wondered what had happened to Jack.

Jamie suddenly broke into tears sobbing loudly. Tobuck consoled her by saying that they will definitely do something. He began packing up the things required and the two set out. Soon the two were in the castle.

They were hunting for Jack when Tobuck suddenly stopped and said "Remember the device that Jack gave to you. You can press the button and it will beep. It will help find Jack." Jamie pressed her device hard. Tobuck suddenly heard some noise. He ran in that direction and Jamie followed him. "Looks, it came from the depth of the stone." "Fool! It is the entrance of the dungeons" said Jamie. Together they heaved the big stone. This was the entrance to the dungeons. The two rushed down the stairs. They found themselves at the place the tunnel started. They took the first tunnel and rushed down inside it.

Meanwhile, what had happened to Jack? He had been dragged down by two of Haidi's men Carl and Tony into the secret chamber where the first tunnel ended. He had been tightly tied to the chair and now was being asked questions about the area of the Palesto castle. He refused to answer them and Haidi was not willing to get into a fight with a stubborn, fighting, rude teenager. So, they left him there, while they went to get a timer bomb. He was sitting alone, thinking he was doomed. His legs hurt after the furious fight. He regretted his harsh decision to come alone. He wished the two were with them. At least, Tobuck could have knocked down the two men while he fought with Haidi. “Pssst! Be quiet. We have come to free you.” And there appeared Tobuck and Jamie’s face. Tobuck freed his bounding and they were about to escape when they got a nasty surprise.

CHAPTER EIGHT

Trapped!!

Haidi Matar was standing behind them. He jumped up and caught Jack and Jamie. Tobuck immediately punched him on his jaw, sending him reeling behind. Haidi immediately took out his revolver and pointed toward Jack. "No!" said Tobuck coldly. He allowed the trio to be tied and to wrap the timer bomb around them. Haidi went away laughing. Jamie burst into tears and sobs. She cried loudly "I don't want to die so soon. Our parents will be very sad...........No! No!"

"Stop it! Here we are trapped and are to be killed and you are just crying madly and thinking about the future," said Tobuck getting irritated.

Jack suddenly jumped up gleefully. He said "Do you see something shining in the corner of the wall near us? It is the broken dagger. If we could reach there somehow I could cut the rope that bound my wrist and the middle portion of my hand Then I could use the hunter's technique to set you all free. After that, I could take my pocket knife and defuse the bomb." It seemed to knock some sense in them.

Tobuck stretched out his legs as far as he could and got the dagger. He passed it to Jack who put his plan into his action. He opened the bomb. On one side was complex machinery and on the other side was a stick of dynamite.

Connecting them was a box. Jack quickly opened the box. He saw two switches. He asked, "Right or left." Jamie said "Left." He clicked on the left switch and closed his eyes. He realized that he had defused the bomb. He had done it. He quickly cut his companions' bounding They ran to the opening of the secret tunnel and had begun their escape.

CHAPTER NINE

A great escape

They had already entered the tunnel when they heard a thud! They froze for a minute and then resumed their escape. Tobuck by mistake looked behind and cried out "The men are behind! Race up!"

"I knew it! They might have realized that the bomb did not explode on time and came to check what was wrong. When they entered they found us not there and rushed to the tunnel to catch us" said Jack panting.

He suddenly stopped. He felt for something in his pocket. He produced a long piece of rope. "You go, Jamie, I and Tobuck are coming in a minute."He and Tobuck held the ends of the rope and stood near the side of the tunnel and crouched down low. When the men came they tripped on the rope and fell heavily.

Jack and Tobuck hurried to Jamie, who was nearly out of the tunnel. Soon, they were out of the dungeons and in the castle. Without wasting even a moment, they rushed to the inn and reached their destination.

Jack dropped down unconscious and had to be dragged till they reached Tobuck's room. Jamie quickly brought a glass of water and sprinkled a few drops of water on his face. Jack started to blink a little and within a minute regained his senses. "Well I am hungry" complained Jack.

Jamie quickly made some sandwiches and the trio had a little feast. Now all the adventure had to be told to Mr. And Mrs. Fenturn.

CHAPTER TEN

A happy ending

They went down to meet Mr. And Mrs. Fenturn. They were waiting for them, looking quite scared. As soon as Mrs. Fenturn saw the trio, she hugged them tightly.

Suddenly Jamie broke into tears. She could not bear the excitement of the adventure. She sobbed "Uncle ....we stopped ...Haidi .....hiding.......castle!!" "I can't understand even a bit. Come in the hall and speak."

They all went into the hall. Jack introduced the story of their whole adventure. Jamie spoke a bit. Mrs. Fenturn got pale when she heard how the timer bomb was attached to them. Tobuck did the ending part. After listening to them, Mr. Fenturn got up and said "I am calling the police, wait a second."After a few minutes on phone, Mr. Fenturn came back and said, "The police are reaching there within seconds. You children enjoy!"

The children passed their time playing cards and watching films. Soon it was time for dinner and the children were having a grand feast. As they were about to sleep, Jack said sleepily "I wish we get another adventure like this."And who knows they might get one!

Thank you

9 798889 516088

Printed by Libri Plureos GmbH in Hamburg, Germany